Hard Times
on the
Prairie

THE LITTLE HOUSE
CHAPTER BOOKS

**Adapted from the Little House books
by Laura Ingalls Wilder
Illustrated by Renée Graef**

A LITTLE HOUSE CHAPTER BOOK

LITTLE HOUSE
The Laura Years

Hard Times
on the
Prairie

Adapted from the Little House books by

LAURA INGALLS WILDER

illustrated by

RENÉE GRAEF

HarperTrophy®
A Division of HarperCollinsPublishers

Adaptation by Melissa Peterson.

Illustrations for this book are inspired by the work of Garth Williams
with his permission, which we gratefully acknowledge.

HarperCollins®, ☕®, HarperTrophy®, and Little House®
are trademarks of HarperCollins Publishers Inc.

Library of Congress Cataloging-in-Publication Data
Wilder, Laura Ingalls, 1867–1957.
   Hard times on the prairie / adapted from the Little house books by Laura
Ingalls Wilder ; illustrated by Renée Graef.
      p.   cm. — (A Little house chapter book)
   Summary: Laura and her pioneer family struggle against hardships on the
Kansas frontier, including a prairie fire, a grasshopper invasion, and a blizzard.
   ISBN 0-06-027792-0 (lib. bdg.) — ISBN 0-06-442077-9 (pbk.)
   1. Wilder, Laura Ingalls, 1867–1957—Juvenile fiction.   [1. Wilder, Laura
Ingalls, 1867–1957—Fiction.   2. Frontier and pioneer life—Kansas—Fiction.
3. Family life—Kansas—Fiction.   4. Kansas—Fiction.]   I. Graef, Renée, ill.
II. Title.   III. Series.
PZ7.W6461Har   1998   97-34351
[Fic]—dc21   CIP
                                                                                AC

❖
First Harper Trophy edition, 1998

Contents

CHAPTER 1

Fire

Spring had come to the Kansas prairie. The air was fresh and crisp. Big white clouds floated in the clear sky. When the prairie was this bright and friendly, it was hard for Laura to remember that there had ever been bad times.

Laura loved her new home on the prairie. Her family had moved there last summer. Laura and her Ma and Pa, and her two sisters, Mary and Carrie, had traveled in a covered wagon all the way from Wisconsin to Kansas.

The trip had been long and tiring. And when they had finally reached the spot that Pa said would be their new home, things hadn't been much easier. The whole family had gotten sick, and a wolf pack had prowled the area all winter. There had been some truly scary moments.

But now the prairie was warm and sunny and sweet. Perhaps the hard times were over.

Pa was out working in the fields. The ground was choked with dry, dead grass. Pa had to plow up all that dead grass before he could plant his crops.

Laura and her big sister, Mary, were in the log cabin helping Ma make dinner. Baby Carrie was playing on the floor in the sunshine. Suddenly the sunshine went away.

Ma looked out the window.

 2

"I do believe it is going to storm," she said.

Laura looked, too. Huge black clouds were rising up from the south and covering the sun.

Pet and Patty, Pa's horses, came running in from the field. They pulled the heavy plow behind them. Pa hung on to the plow with all his might, bounding in great leaps to keep up with the horses.

"Prairie fire!" he shouted.

Laura swallowed hard. Fire!

Pa was still shouting. "Get the tub full of water! Put sacks in it! Hurry!"

Ma ran to the well, and Laura dragged the washtub over. Pa hurried to put the cow and calf into the stable. He came out with an armful of old sacks and flung them on the ground.

Laura snatched up the sacks and took

3

them to Ma at the well. Ma was pulling up buckets of water as fast as she could. The sky was black now. It was as dark as night.

Pa ran back to the plow. He shouted at Pet and Patty to make them hurry. He wanted to plow a ditch around the house. If the ditch was wide enough, the fire wouldn't be able to jump over it and reach the house.

But there wasn't enough time. Pa plowed a long furrow around three sides of the house. Then he tied Pet and Patty to the far corner.

"I couldn't plow but one furrow," he panted. "Hurry, Caroline. That fire's coming faster than a horse can run."

The tub was almost full of water. Laura helped Ma push the sacks under the water to soak them.

 4

Rabbits were leaping past them as if they weren't even there. One big rabbit jumped right over the washtub. Ma told Laura to stay by the house. Pa and Ma lifted the heavy tub and carried it to the furrow Pa had plowed.

From the house Laura could see the red fire coming under billows of smoke. More rabbits went bounding by. They paid no attention to Jack, the bulldog. Jack didn't even try to chase them. He just crowded close to Laura and whined.

The wind was rising. The smoke blew closer. Thousands of birds flew ahead of the fire. Thousands of rabbits were running. All the prairie animals were trying to get away from the fire.

Pa was going along the furrow he had plowed, setting fire to the grass on the other side. He was making a little fire to

5

keep the big fire away from the house. Ma followed him with a wet sack. She beat at the flames that tried to cross the furrow.

Soon Pa's little fire was all around the house. He helped Ma fight it with wet sacks. They mustn't let any of those little flames jump over the ditch to the house side. Whenever a flame got across the furrow, Pa and Ma stamped on it with their feet. They ran back and forth in the smoke, fighting the fire.

The big prairie fire was roaring closer. Huge flames flared and twisted high. The rolling black smoke clouds glowed red above the wall of fire. The flames were moving across the prairie, right toward the house.

Laura and Mary stood against the house and trembled. Baby Carrie was inside. Laura wanted to do something, but there

 6

was nothing to do. Her eyes stung from the smoke.

Jack howled. The horses squealed with fright. They jerked and pulled at their ropes. Firelight flickered over the grass and the house and the horses.

Pa's little fire had made a burned black strip. Slowly the little fire crawled to meet the racing big fire. And suddenly the big fire swallowed the little one.

The wind rose to a high, rushing wail. Flames climbed into the crackling air. Fire was all around the house.

Then it was over.

The fire went roaring past the house and away across the prairie. There were little flames here and there in the yard. But Ma and Pa beat them out with wet sacks.

When all the flames were out, Ma came

 8

to the house to wash her hands. She was streaked with smoke and sweat. But she said there was nothing to worry about now.

"The little fire saved us," she said. "All's well that ends well."

The air smelled scorched. As far as Laura could see, the prairie was burned and black. Ashes blew on the wind. Smoke rose from the scorched grasses. Everything felt different.

But Pa and Ma were cheerful. The fire was gone, and it had not done them any harm. It had not missed them by much, Pa said, but a miss was as good as a mile.

CHAPTER 2

The Footbridge

The prairie fire cleared the ground and made it easier for Pa to plow. Soon the Kansas prairie was green and beautiful again. Laura liked Kansas. She was sad when Pa decided to move the family to Minnesota. But in Minnesota they found a nice farm near a creek called Plum Creek.

They moved into a funny little house called a dugout. The dugout was built right into the side of a hill. The walls were dirt and the floor was dirt. The roof was prairie grass that waved in the wind.

Laura liked their new home even more than their home in Kansas. She especially loved the creek and the willow trees that grew near it. Laura and Mary played in the creek all summer.

But one night Laura awoke to a terrible roaring sound. She had never heard anything so loud.

"Pa! Pa, what's that?" she cried.

"Sounds like the creek," he answered. He jumped out of bed and opened the door. The roaring sound filled the house.

"Jiminy crickets!" Pa shouted. "It's raining fishhooks and hammer handles!"

He said they didn't need to worry, though—the creek would not rise as high as the house. But even with the door shut, the roaring sound was everywhere. Laura had a hard time getting back to sleep.

When she woke up, it was morning. Pa

11

was gone. Ma was fixing breakfast, and the creek was still roaring.

In a flash Laura was out of bed and opening the door. Whoosh! Icy-cold rain soaked her to the skin. It took her breath away. Right at her feet, the creek was rushing and roaring.

There used to be a path with steps right outside the door. The steps led to a little bridge, which was a wide plank that crossed the creek. But today the footbridge was hidden under the angry, churning water. Laura stared at the water. It swallowed the young willow trees right up to their tops. It was fast and strong and terrible.

Suddenly Ma jerked Laura into the dugout.

"Didn't you hear me call you?" she asked.

"No, Ma," said Laura.

"Well, no," Ma said, "I suppose you didn't."

Water was streaming down Laura and making a puddle around her bare feet. Ma told her to put on dry clothes before she caught cold. But Laura was glowing warm inside.

"Oh, Mary," she cried, "you just ought to see the creek! Ma, may I go out and see it again after breakfast?"

"You may not!" said Ma. "Not while it is raining."

During breakfast, the rain stopped. Pa said that Laura and Mary might go with him to look at the creek.

The air was fresh and clean. Up on the high bank, Laura could still hear the creek roaring. Everything looked different after the storm. Where there had been a thicket of plum trees, now there was only foamy wood in the water. The gentle creek was swollen into a wide, churning river.

The next day the creek was still roaring, but more softly. Laura was sure that Ma would not let her go to play in it. So she quietly slipped outdoors without saying anything to Ma.

The water was not so high now. It had gone down from the steps leading to the footbridge, and part of the bridge showed above the water.

Laura took off her shoes and stockings. She put them safely on the bottom step. Then she walked out on the plank and stood watching the noisy water.

Drops splashed her bare feet. Little waves ran over the plank. Laura poked one foot into the swirling water.

She sat down on the plank and let her

 14

legs dangle into the water. The creek ran strong against them. She loved the feel of the pushing water.

Now she was wet almost all over. But only almost. Her whole skin wanted to be in the water. She lay on her stomach and thrust her arms deep into the fast current.

But that was not enough. The creek was usually quiet and still. Today it was noisy and joyous. It bubbled and laughed to itself. She really wanted to be in that roaring, laughing water.

She locked her hands under the plank and rolled off it.

In an instant she knew the creek was not playing. It was strong and terrible. It grabbed her whole body and pulled her under the plank. Only her head was out, and one arm holding on tight.

The water was pulling her and pushing her. Her chin held on to the edge. Her arm clutched the board, while the water pulled at all the rest of her.

The creek was not laughing now.

No one knew where she was. If she screamed for help, no one would hear. The water tugged at her, stronger and stronger. Laura kicked, but the water was stronger than her legs.

She got both arms across the plank and pulled. The water pulled harder. It was cold. The coldness soaked into her.

 16

If she let go, the creek would toss her like a willow branch. Her legs were tired, and her arms hardly felt the plank anymore.

"I must get out. I must!" she thought. She heard the creek roaring in her head. She kicked hard with both feet and pulled hard with her arms. Then— *whump!*—she was lying on the plank again.

She lay against the rough plank and felt how solid it was. She stayed there awhile, feeling the good solid wood beneath her.

When she moved, her head whirled. She crawled off the plank. She took her shoes and stockings and climbed slowly up the muddy steps.

She didn't know what she would say to Ma. When she went inside, she just stood still in the doorway, dripping.

Ma looked up from her sewing.

"Where have you been, Laura?" she

asked. "My goodness!"

She began unbuttoning Laura's soaking wet dress.

"What happened? Did you fall in the creek?"

"No, ma'am," Laura said. "I—I went in."

Ma listened as Laura explained and went on undressing her. She rubbed Laura all over with a warm towel. She did not say a word.

Laura finished telling Ma what had happened, and still Ma did not say anything. Laura's teeth chattered. Ma wrapped her in a quilt and sat her close to the stove.

At last Ma said, "Well, Laura, you have been very naughty. I think you knew it all the time. But I can't punish you. I can't even scold you. You came near to being drowned."

Laura did not say anything.

"You won't go near the creek again till Pa or I say you may, and that won't be till the water goes down," said Ma.

"No, ma'am," Laura said.

The creek would go down. It would be a nice place to play again. But nobody could make it do that. Nobody could make it do anything.

Laura knew now that some things were stronger than anybody.

But the creek had not got her. It had not made her scream, and it could not make her cry.

CHAPTER 3

Ox on the Roof

On top of the dugout house was the prairie, and out on the prairie was a large gray rock. One evening Laura and Mary sat on the rock waiting for Pete and Bright, Pa's big oxen, to come home. Pa was working in town, and Pete and Bright had no work to do until Pa was finished. They spent their days with other cattle, out where the grass was long and green.

Laura and Mary waited on the rock, just as they did every evening. Jack, the bulldog, lay in the grass at their feet. He was waiting, too.

Suddenly Laura heard a great bellowing. The cattle were coming—and they were angry! When they reached the gray rock, the herd did not go by as it usually did. The cattle ran around the rock, bawling and fighting. Their eyes rolled. Their horns slashed at one another.

The air was choked with dust raised by their kicking hooves. Mary was so scared that she couldn't move. Laura was scared, too—so scared that she jumped right off the rock.

She knew she had to drive Pete and Bright into the stable. The cattle towered up in the dust.

Behind them ran Johnny Johnson. He was the boy who looked after the herd. Johnny tried to head Pete and Bright in the right direction. Trampling hooves and slashing horns were everywhere.

21

Jack jumped up. He ran toward the cattle, growling at their hooves. Laura ran, yelling, behind them.

Johnny waved his big stick. He managed to drive the rest of the herd away. Jack and Laura chased Bright into the stable. Pete was going in, too. Laura was not so scared now.

And then, in a flash, big Pete wheeled around. His horns hooked and his tail stood straight up. He galloped after the herd.

Laura ran in front of Pete to head him off. She waved her arms and yelled. Pete bellowed. He went thundering toward the creek bank.

Laura ran with all her might. She had to get in front of Pete again, to turn him back. But her legs were short and Pete's were long. The big ox raced ahead.

Jack came running as fast as he could. Pete ran faster and jumped longer jumps. And—*thump!* He jumped right on top of the dugout.

Laura saw one of his hind legs go down through the roof. Pete was going to fall right on Ma and Carrie! Laura ran even faster.

Finally she was in front of Pete. Jack ran like lightning. He circled in front of the huge ox.

Pete heaved and pulled his leg out of the hole. Before he could do any more damage, Laura and Jack chased him off the roof. They chased him into the stable, and Laura put up the bars that kept him inside.

Laura was shaking all over. Her legs were weak and her knees knocked against each other.

But no harm had been done. There was only a hole in the dugout roof where Pete's hoof had gone through. Ma stuffed it with some hay, and that was that.

CHAPTER 4

Grasshoppers

That summer Pa moved the family from the dugout to a new house he had built for them. The house was made of straight, beautiful boards. It had two rooms and an attic, where Laura and Mary would sleep. It even had glass windows!

Down the little hill from the wonderful house was Pa's wheat field. The wheat was almost ready to cut. Every day Pa looked at it. Every night he talked about it. Pa said the weather was perfect for ripening wheat.

One morning Pa took Laura with him to look at the wheat. It was almost as tall as Pa. He lifted her onto his shoulder so that she could see. Laura looked all around at the heavy, bending tops of the wheat. The field was greeny gold.

At the dinner table Pa told Ma about it. He had never seen such a crop. When that crop was harvested, Pa said, they'd be out of debt. It had cost a lot of money to build a new house. But after Pa sold this fine wheat crop, they'd have more money than they knew what to do with.

Pa would get a buggy. Ma would have a silk dress. They'd all get new shoes, and they'd eat beef every Sunday.

The weather was very hot. The prairie felt like a big stove. They ate dinner with the door open, and the afternoon sunshine streamed in. Suddenly something seemed to dim the sunshine. Laura rubbed her eyes and looked again.

The sunshine really was dim. It grew dimmer until there was no sunshine at all.

"I do believe a storm is coming up," Ma said. "There must be a cloud over the sun."

Pa got up quickly and went outside. A storm might hurt the wheat.

The light was strange. It did not seem like the light before a storm. Laura was scared, and she didn't know why.

She ran outdoors. Pa stood looking up at the sky. Ma and Mary came out, too.

Pa asked, "What do you make of that, Caroline?"

A cloud was over the sun. It was not like any cloud they had seen before. It was a cloud of something like snowflakes, but they were bigger than snowflakes. They were thin and glittering.

Plunk! Something hit Laura's head and fell to the ground. It was the largest grasshopper she had ever seen.

Then huge brown grasshoppers were hitting the ground all around her. They came thudding down like hail.

The whole cloud was grasshoppers! Their bodies hid the sun and made darkness. Their thin wings glittered and made a rasping sound that filled the whole air.

Laura tried to beat them off, but they clung to her skin and her dress. Mary ran into the house. Grasshoppers covered the ground.

Ma was slamming the windows shut all around the house. Grasshoppers plunked onto the roof, making a sound as loud as hailstones hitting it.

 28

Then Laura heard another sound.

It was one big sound of tiny nips and snips and chewings.

"The wheat!" Pa shouted. He dashed out the door and ran to the wheat field.

The grasshoppers were eating. Millions of jaws were biting and chewing. They ate all the short grass off the hill. They ate the tall, waving prairie grasses. They ate the leaves off the willow trees.

The green garden rows were disappearing. The grasshoppers ate the potatoes, the carrots, the beets, and the beans. They munched the long leaves off the cornstalks. They crunched the tender young kernels of corn in the husks.

Pa lit fires around the wheat field, hoping the smoke would keep the grasshoppers away. Smoke hid the field, and Laura could hardly see Pa on the other side.

Ma sent Laura to bring in the cow for milking. Laura wrapped herself in a shawl to keep the grasshoppers off her. But the grasshoppers swarmed over her and crawled right under the shawl. She swatted them off her face and hands.

The cow swished her tail angrily to keep the grasshoppers away. When Ma milked her, they could not keep the grasshoppers out of the milk. Ma skimmed them out with a tin cup.

Pa stayed in the fields all night. In bed Laura and Mary could still hear the whirring and snipping and chewing. There were no grasshoppers in bed, but Laura could not get rid of the feeling of little legs crawling on her.

The next morning the whole prairie had changed. The grasses had fallen in ridges. The willow trees were bare. There

were no more plums on the plum trees, and no leaves either. Laura could still hear the sound of the grasshoppers eating.

At noon Pa came slowly out of the smoky wheat field. His face was black and his eyes were red from the smoke.

"It's no use, Caroline," he said. "Smoke won't stop them. They keep dropping down through it and hopping in from all sides. The wheat is falling now. They're eating it, straw and all."

The grasshoppers ate every bit of the wheat. Day after day they kept on eating. They ate the oats Pa had planted for the horses. They ate every green thing that grew in the fields and the garden and on the prairie.

"Oh, Pa, what will the rabbits do?" Laura asked. "And the poor birds?"

"Look around you, Laura," said Pa.

 32

The rabbits had all gone away. Most of the birds were gone. The birds that were left were eating grasshoppers. Prairie hens ran with their necks stuck out, gobbling grasshoppers down.

Laura hated to walk anywhere. She could not stand to have grasshoppers crunching under her bare feet. And she had to save her shoes for winter now. There would be no new shoes for anyone, and no buggy for Pa, no silk dress for Ma. Laura remembered that the house was not paid for. Pa had said he would pay for it when he harvested the wheat.

But Pa said not to worry. "We did all we could," he told them, "and we'll pull through somehow."

He began to plow the bare wheat field, to make it ready for next year's crop.

CHAPTER 5

Eggs

One day later that summer, Laura and Jack wandered down to the creek. It was almost dry. Only a little water seeped through the sand. The bare willow branches stuck up above the footbridge. The dry earth was hot, and the whirring of grasshoppers sounded like heat.

Suddenly Laura noticed something odd. All over the ground, grasshoppers were sitting still with their tails in the dirt. They did not move, even when Laura poked them.

She pushed one away from the hole it

was sitting in. With a stick she dug something out of the hole. It was gray and shaped like a worm. But it was not alive. She didn't know what it was. Jack sniffed at it.

Laura started toward the wheat field to ask Pa about it. But Pa was not plowing. He was staring at the ground.

Then Laura saw him lift the plow out of its furrow. He drove the horses toward the stable. Laura knew that only something dreadful would make Pa stop work in the middle of the day.

She hurried to the stable. The horses were in their stalls, and Pa was hanging up their harness. He did not smile at Laura when he saw her. She tagged slowly after him into the house.

Ma looked up and said, "Charles! What is the matter now?"

"The grasshoppers are laying their eggs," Pa said. "All over the wheat field. Everywhere. You can't put your finger down between them. Look here."

He took something out of his pocket. It was a gray thing just like the one Laura had found.

"That's one of 'em," Pa said. "A pod of grasshopper eggs. I've been cutting them open. There are thirty-five or forty eggs in every pod. There's a pod in every hole. There are eight or ten holes to the square foot. All over this whole country."

Ma dropped down in a chair. Her hands fell helpless at her sides.

"We've got no more chance of making a crop next year than we have of flying," said Pa. "When those eggs hatch, there won't be a green thing in this part of the world."

"Oh, Charles!" Ma said. "What will we do?"

Pa slumped down on a bench.

"I don't know," he said.

Mary came to stand close beside Laura. They did not say a word. They only looked at each other. They looked at Pa.

Suddenly Pa sat up straight. His eyes brightened with a fierce light. It was not like the twinkle Laura had always seen in them.

"I do know this, Caroline," Pa said. "No pesky mess of grasshoppers can beat us! We'll get along somehow."

"Yes, Charles," said Ma.

"Why not?" said Pa. "We're healthy, we've got a roof over our heads. We're better off than lots of folks. I'll find something to do. Don't you worry!"

That night Pa went to town, and when

he came back, he had a plan. About a hundred miles to the east, there were no grasshoppers. Beyond that, there were crops. And it was harvest time. Pa would walk the hundred miles and get a job out there.

After breakfast the next day, Pa kissed them all and went away. He took his extra shirt and a pair of socks. Just before he crossed Plum Creek, he looked back and waved. Then he went on, all the way out of sight.

Laura and Mary and Ma stood still for a moment after he was gone. Then Ma smiled a cheerful smile.

"We have to take care of everything now, girls," she said. "Mary and Laura, you hurry with the cow to meet the herd."

She went briskly into the house with Carrie. Laura and Mary ran to let the cow out of the stable and drive her toward the creek. No prairie grass was left for the cows to eat. The hungry cattle had to wander along the creek banks, eating willow sprouts and plum brush.

Everything was flat and dull when Pa was gone. Laura and Mary could not even count the days till he would come back. They could only think of him walking farther and farther away.

Plum Creek dried up. There were no leaves on the trees. The only shade was in the house. The grasshoppers had eaten everything.

Weeks passed. The weather turned cold. And one day, at last, the long wait was over. Pa came home. He had earned enough money to buy new boots for himself and new shoes and dresses for the girls. He was home in time for Christmas, and Laura was so happy, she forgot all about the grasshoppers.

There was not much snow that winter. Spring came early. A warm wind blew in from the northwest and melted all the snow. Plum Creek was full again. Spring rains brought out new green leaves on the willows and the plum trees. Laura and Mary and even Carrie ran barefooted over the soft grass.

Every day was warmer than the day before, till hot summer came.

 40

One day when Pa came in for dinner, he said, "The grasshoppers are hatching. This hot sun is bringing them out of the eggs like corn popping."

Laura ran out to see. The grass was full of tiny green things. Laura caught one. Its little wings and legs and head were the color of grass. It was tiny and perfect. Laura could hardly believe it would ever be a big, brown, ugly grasshopper.

"They'll be big fast enough," said Pa. "Eating every growing thing."

Day by day more grasshoppers hatched. They swarmed everywhere, eating. It was just like the year before. They ate all the young plants coming up in the garden. They ate the grass, the willow leaves, and the plums. Once again the prairie turned bare and brown. The fierce sun beat down and baked the bare ground.

The grasshoppers grew. They became large and brown and ugly. The sound of their chewing was all Laura could hear. Every bit of ground was covered with grasshoppers. Laura and Mary stayed in the house.

"Oh, Charles," Ma said one morning. "Seems to me I just can't bear one more day of this."

Pa did not say anything. He walked to the door and stood looking out. Even Carrie was still. They were all quiet, listening to the grasshoppers.

But this morning, the grasshoppers were making a new sound. Laura ran to look at them.

"Caroline!" Pa said. "Here's a strange thing. Come look!"

All across the yard, the grasshoppers

 42

were walking. They were in one big crowd, shoulder to shoulder and end to end. Not a single one hopped. As fast as they could go, they were all walking west.

"Oh, Pa, what does it mean?" asked Mary.

"I don't know," Pa said. He shaded his eyes and looked across the prairie. "It's the same, as far as the eye can see. The whole ground is crawling."

They all stood looking at that strange sight. Only Carrie wasn't interested. She sat in her chair, beating the table with her spoon.

"Ma, Ma!" she shouted.

"There, you shall have your breakfast," Ma said, turning around. Then she cried out, "My goodness!"

Grasshoppers were walking over Carrie. They came pouring in the eastern window.

Side by side, row after row, the grass-hoppers walked across the floor from east to west. They walked under the table and over it. They went right up the legs of Carrie's chair and walked across the top of her head.

"Shut the window!" Ma cried.

Laura ran to close it. Quickly they closed the upstairs windows as well. Ma and Laura swept up grasshoppers and threw them out the western window.

That whole day the grasshoppers walked west. All the next day they kept on walking, and the day after that. No grasshopper turned out of its way for any-thing.

The fourth day came and the grasshoppers went on walking. It was nearly noon when Pa came from the stable shouting, "Caroline! The grasshoppers are flying!"

 44

Laura and Mary ran to the door. Everywhere, grasshoppers were spreading their wings and rising from the ground. More and more of them filled the air. They flew higher and higher, until the sunshine dimmed, the way it had dimmed the day the grasshoppers came.

Laura ran outside. She looked up at the cloud of grasshoppers. It glittered and moved across the sun. It went on far to the west until she could not see it anymore.

There was not a grasshopper left. The air was empty, and the ground was still. It was like the stillness after a storm.

Ma went into the house and sank into the rocking chair.

"My Lord!" she said. "My Lord!" The words were praying, but they sounded like "Thank you!"

CHAPTER 6

Snow

The next winter there was so much snow, it was hard to remember the grasshoppers and the hot, dry days of summer. When the snow blew so thick, it was easy to get lost. Once, when Pa went to the stable to do the chores, he almost walked right past the stable out onto the open prairie. He might have wandered for miles in the freezing snow if he hadn't bumped into the stable by accident. Now Pa stretched a rope between the house and the stable to guide himself.

One blizzard raged for three days.

When at last it died down, Pa decided to take a trip to town.

"I need some tobacco for my pipe and I want to hear the news," he said. He filled up the woodbox before he left. Ma was worried about the cold. She made him put on an extra pair of socks, to keep his feet from getting frostbitten.

"I do wish you had a buffalo overcoat," Ma said. "That old coat is worn so thin."

"And I wish you had some diamonds," said Pa. "Don't you worry, Caroline."

Pa smiled at them while he buckled the belt of his old, thin coat. He put on his warm felt hat and said a cheery good-bye.

The house was quiet without him. But Laura and Mary were busy with chores, and it was noon before they knew it. It was time for Pa to come home. The beans were cooked and the bread was baked. Everything was ready for Pa's dinner.

Laura looked out the window. Something was wrong with the sunshine.

"Ma!" she cried. "The sun is a funny color."

Ma looked up from her sewing, startled. She went quickly to the window. Then she said, "Girls, bundle up and bring in more wood. If Pa hasn't started home, he will stay in town, and we will need more wood in the house."

Mary and Laura hurried out to the woodpile. They could see a dark cloud coming. There was barely time to get an armload of wood into the house before the storm came howling. Snow whirled so thickly that they could not see the doorstep.

"That will do for now," Ma said. "The

storm can't get much worse, and Pa may come in a few minutes."

Mary and Laura took off their coats and warmed their hands. They waited for Pa.

He didn't come.

The wind howled around the house. Snow swished against the windows. The black hands of the clock moved slowly around its face.

At two o'clock, Ma dished up three bowls of beans. "Here, girls," she said. "You might as well eat your dinner. Pa must have stayed in town."

The storm was growing worse. The house shook in the wind. Snow blew in around the windows that Pa had made so tight.

At last Ma said she had better do the chores. Pa would surely stay in town all night now. Ma bundled up warm. She put on Pa's old boots. Her small feet were lost in them, but they would keep out the snow.

"May I go with you, Ma?" Laura asked.

"No," said Ma. "Now listen to me. Be careful of fire. Nobody but Mary is to touch the stove, no matter how long I am gone. Nobody is to go outdoors, or even open a door, till I come back."

Then she hung the milk pail on her arm and went outside. She reached through the whirling snow till she got hold of the rope Pa had hung. She shut the back door behind her.

Laura ran to the window, but she could not see Ma. She could see nothing but snow. The wind howled.

Laura thought of Ma, out in that storm. Ma would go step by step, holding on to the line. She could not see anything at all

in the whirling snow, but the rope would
keep her safe. Laura and Mary and Carrie
waited by the fire. Laura could hardly sit
still, thinking about Ma alone out there in
that whirling snow.

But at last the door blew open, and
there was Ma. She was covered with snow,
and her hands were stiff with cold. Laura
had to untie Ma's hood. Mary took the

milk pail, and Ma asked, "Is there any milk left?"

There was just a little milk in the bottom of the pail. The wind had blown most of it out of the pail on Ma's walk back to the house.

"The wind is terrible," Ma said. She warmed her hands. Then she lighted the lamp and set it on the windowsill.

"Why are you doing that, Ma?" Mary asked.

Ma said, "Don't you think the lamplight's pretty, shining against the snow outside?"

After Ma had rested, they ate their supper of bread and milk. Then they all sat still by the stove and listened. They heard the wind shrieking, and the house creaking, and the snow swishing.

"This will never do!" said Ma. "Let's

 52

play bean-porridge hot! Mary, you and Laura play it together, and Carrie, you hold up your hands. We'll do it faster than Laura and Mary can!"

So they all played bean-porridge hot, faster and faster. Soon they were laughing so hard they could not say the rhymes.

But after a while it was bedtime, and they could hear the storm howling around the quiet house again. Ma kissed them good night. Mary climbed the ladder to the attic bedroom she shared with Laura. But Laura stopped halfway up the ladder. She asked Ma, "Pa did stay in town, didn't he?"

Ma's voice was cheerful. "Why, surely, Laura. No doubt he and Mr. Fitch are sitting by the stove right now, telling stories and cracking jokes."

Laura went to bed. Deep in the night she woke. She saw lamplight shining from

53

the hole where the ladder came up through the floor. She crept out of bed and looked down through the hole.

Ma sat alone in her chair. Her head was bowed and she was very still. Her eyes were open, looking at her hands clasped in her lap. The lamp was shining in the window.

For a long time Laura looked down. Ma did not move. The lamp went on shining.

CHAPTER 7

Day of Games

The next day the storm was even wilder. Upstairs, it was so cold that Laura couldn't stand to get dressed. She grabbed her clothes and hurried downstairs to dress by the stove.

Ma went out to do the chores. This time she took even longer than the day before. When she came back, her skirt was frozen stiff with ice. She had drawn water from the well for the horses and cows. The wind had flung the water on her clothes, and the water had frozen quickly in the cold. Ma hardly had time to thaw and rest

55

before she had to go back outside for wood. Mary and Laura begged her to let them bring it.

"No," Ma said. "You girls are not big enough, and you'd be lost. You do not know what this storm is like. I'll get the wood. You open the door for me."

Laura and Mary opened and shut the door for her. Ma piled wood high on the woodbox. Then she rested, and they mopped up the puddles of snow melting from the wood.

"You are good girls," Ma said. She looked around and praised them for keeping the house so neat while she was gone. Mary and Laura sat down to study their lessons, but it was hard to think about anything except Pa.

"I don't believe we want lessons, girls!" Ma said. "Suppose we don't do anything today but play. Think what we'll play first. Pussy-in-the-corner! Would you like that?"

"Oh yes!" they said.

Laura stood in one corner, Mary in another, and Carrie in a third. There were only three corners because the stove was in one. Ma stood in the middle of the floor and cried, "Poor pussy wants a corner!"

Then all at once they ran out of their corners and each tried to get into another corner. Everyone was excited, even Jack. Ma dodged into Mary's corner. That left Mary out to be poor pussy. Then Laura fell over Jack, and that left Laura out. Carrie ran laughing into the wrong corners at first, but she soon learned.

They all ran till they were gasping from running and shouting and laughing. They had to rest.

"Bring me the slate," said Ma, "and I'll tell you a story."

"Why do you need a slate to tell a story?" Laura asked.

"You'll see," said Ma.

This is the story she told:

Far in the woods there was a pond, like this:

The pond was full of fishes, like this:

Down below the pond lived two homesteaders, each in a little tent, because they had not built their houses yet:

They went often to the pond to fish, and they made crooked paths:

A little way from the pond lived an old man and an old woman in a little house with a window:

One day the old woman went to
    the pond to get a pail of water:
And she saw the fishes all flying
        out of the pond, like this:
The old woman ran back as fast
as she could go, to tell the old
man, "All the fishes are flying
out of the pond!" The old man
stuck his long nose out of the
        house to have a good look:
And he said: "Pshaw! It's nothing
but tadpoles!"

"It's a bird!" Carrie yelled. She clapped
her hands and laughed till she rolled off
the footstool.

Laura and Mary laughed too and
begged Ma to tell another.

"Well, if I must," said Ma, and she
began, "This is the house that Jack built

for two pieces of money."

She covered both sides of the slate with the pictures of that story. Ma let Mary and Laura read it and look at the pictures as long as they liked. Then Ma asked, "Mary, can you tell that story?"

"Yes!" said Mary.

Ma wiped the slate clean and gave it to Mary.

"Write it on the slate, then," she said. "And Laura and Carrie, I have new play-things for you."

She gave her thimble to Laura, and she got out Mary's thimble for Carrie. She showed them that pressing the thimbles into the frost on the windows made per-fect circles. They could make pictures on the windows!

Laura used the thimble circles to make a Christmas tree. She made birds flying.

She made a log house with smoke coming out of the chimney. She even made a roly-poly man and a roly-poly woman.

Carrie just made circles.

When Laura finished her window and Mary looked up from the slate, the room was dusky. Ma smiled at them.

"We have been so busy, we forgot all about dinner," she said. "Come eat your suppers now."

"Don't you have to do the chores first?" Laura asked.

"Not tonight," said Ma. "It was so late when I fed the animals this morning that I gave them enough to last till tomorrow. Maybe the storm will not be so bad then."

She lighted the lamp, but she did not set it in the window.

"Come eat your suppers now," she said again, "and then we'll all go to bed."

CHAPTER 8

Lost—and Found

The next day the storm was worse than ever. The snow struck the windows with an icy rattle. Pa did not come. It was a long, dark day. That night Laura huddled under her quilt next to Mary to stay warm.

The next morning was even colder. Ma told them not to worry about the housework. They wrapped up in shawls and kept close to the stove.

And then there came a yellow glow through the icy window. Laura scratched away a little ice to make a peephole. She

 62

looked through the hole and saw sunshine!

Laura stared at the pale sunlight. The wind was still blowing waves of snow across the ground. Laura saw something dark moving toward the house. A big furry animal was wading deep in the blowing snow. A bear, Laura thought. She yelled for Ma.

The door opened, and the bear came right inside the house! Pa's blue eyes looked out of its face. Pa's voice said, "Have you been good girls while I was gone?"

Ma ran to him. Laura and Mary and Carrie ran, crying and laughing.

Ma helped Pa out of his coat. Snow flew out of the fur onto the floor.

"Charles!" Ma cried. "You're frozen!"

"Just about," said Pa. "And I'm hungry as a wolf."

He sat down by the fire to eat some of Ma's good bean broth. Ma pulled off his boots, and he put his feet up to the heat from the oven.

"Charles," Ma asked. "Did you— Were you—" She was trembling.

"Now, Caroline, don't you ever worry about me," said Pa. "I'm bound to come home to take care of you and the girls."

His hair and his beard were wet from the melting snow. Ma dried them with a towel. Pa took her hand.

"Caroline, do you know what this weather means?" he asked. "It means we'll have a bumper crop of wheat next year! They say in town that grasshoppers come only when the summers are hot and dry and the winters mild. We are getting so much snow now that we're bound to have fine crops next year."

"That's good, Charles," Ma said.

"They were talking about all this in the store, but I knew I ought to start home. Just as I was leaving, Fitch showed me the buffalo coat. He said I could have the coat for ten dollars. Ten dollars is a lot of money, but—"

"I'm glad you got the coat, Charles," said Ma.

"As it turned out, it's lucky I did, though I didn't know it then."

Mary and Laura and Carrie crowded close while Pa told his story. He had put the furry buffalo coat on over his old, worn coat. As soon as he got out on the prairie, he saw the storm cloud in the sky. He thought he could beat it home, but he was only halfway there when the storm struck.

"I couldn't see my hand before my face," he told them. He tried to walk in the right direction, but the blizzard winds blew snow in his face from all sides. After a while he knew he was lost.

"I had come a good two miles without getting to the creek, and I had no idea which way to turn. The only thing to do was keep on going. I had to walk till the storm quit. If I stopped, I'd freeze."

Pa had walked and walked until the

white snow turned gray and then black. He knew it was night.

"I had the lamp burning in the window for you," Ma said.

"I didn't see it. I kept straining my eyes to see something, but all I saw was dark. Then all of a sudden, everything gave way under me and I went straight down, must have been ten feet."

Pa had walked off the bank of a gully. Snow was piled up all around him, but the side of the bank made a cozy spot protected from the wind. With the buffalo coat to keep him from freezing, Pa was snug as a bear in a den.

"My, I was glad I had that coat!" he said. "And a good warm cap with earlaps, and that extra pair of thick socks, Caroline." His eyes twinkled. "When I woke up, I could hear the blizzard, but faintly. There was solid snow in front of me, coated over with ice where my breath had melted it. There must have been six feet of snow over me, but the air was good. I moved my arms and legs and fingers and toes, and felt my nose and ears to make sure I was not freezing. I could still hear the storm, so I went back to sleep. How long has it been, Caroline?"

"Three days and nights," Ma said. "This is the fourth day."

Then Pa asked Mary and Laura, "Do you know what day it is?"

"Is it Sunday?" Mary guessed.

"It's the day before Christmas," said Ma.

Laura and Mary had forgotten all about Christmas! They had been so worried about Pa. Laura asked, "Did you sleep all that time, Pa?"

"No," said Pa. "I kept on sleeping and waking up hungry, and sleeping some more, till I woke up just about starved. I was bringing home some oyster crackers for Christmas. I took a handful of those crackers and ate them."

He had eaten snow for a drink, and then all he could do was sit and wait. He waited a whole night, and still the storm blew on. After a while he ate the rest of the crackers. But he was still too hungry to sleep.

"Girls," he said, "I was bound and determined I would not do it, but after some time I did. I took the paper bag out of the inside pocket of my old overcoat, and I ate every bit of the Christmas candy. I'm sorry."

Laura hugged him from one side, and Mary hugged him from the other.

"Oh, Pa," said Laura, "I am so glad you did!"

"So am I, Pa! So am I!" said Mary.

"Was it good, Pa?" asked Laura. "Did you feel better after you ate it?"

"It was very good, and I felt much better," said Pa. "I went right to sleep. I must have slept most of yesterday and last night. Suddenly I sat up wide awake. I could not hear a sound."

Pa knew that the silence meant the storm was over. He began to dig with his hands. Like a badger he dug through the snow and came out of the snowbank into the open air.

"And where do you suppose I was?" he asked. "I was on the bank of Plum Creek, just above the place where we set the fish trap!"

"Why, I can see that place from the window," said Laura.

"Yes," said Pa, "and I could see this house."

70

All that long, terrible time he had been so close. The blizzard had hidden the lamp shining in the window. Pa had not seen its light.

"I started for home just as fast as I could go. And here I am!" he finished, hugging Laura and Mary.

Then he went to the big buffalo coat and took a tin can out of a pocket.

"What do you think I have brought you for Christmas dinner?" he asked.

They could not guess.

"Oysters!" Pa said. "Nice, fresh oysters! They were frozen solid when I got them, and they are frozen solid yet. Better put them in the lean-to, Caroline, so they will stay that way till tomorrow."

Laura touched the can. It was cold as ice.

"I ate up the oyster crackers, and I ate

up the Christmas candy," said Pa, "but by jinks, I brought the oysters home!"

Wood shifted and crackled inside the black stove. Pa's eyes twinkled at Mary and Laura and Ma. His blue eyes were warmer than the warm stove. Christmas was still a day away, but to Laura it felt like a holiday now.

It was just as Ma always said. All was well that ended well.

The LAURA *Years*
By Laura Ingalls Wilder
Illustrated by Garth Williams

———————

The ROSE *Years*
By Roger Lea MacBride
Illustrated by Dan Andreasen
& David Gilleece

———————

The CAROLINE *Years*
By Maria D. Wilkes
Illustrated by Dan Andreasen

———————

LAURA INGALLS WILDER was born in 1867 in the log cabin described in LITTLE HOUSE IN THE BIG WOODS. As her classic Little House books tell us, she and her family traveled by covered wagon across the Midwest. She and her husband, Almanzo Wilder, made their own covered-wagon trip with their daughter, Rose, to Mansfield, Missouri. There Laura wrote her story in the Little House books and lived until she was ninety years old. For millions of readers, however, she lives forever as the little pioneer girl in the beloved Little House books.

RENÉE GRAEF received her bachelor's degree in art from the University of Wisconsin at Madison. She is the illustrator of the paper dolls and the Kirsten books in the American Girls Collection, as well as numerous titles in the new Little House publishing program. She lives in Milwaukee, Wisconsin, with her husband, Tim, and their children, Maggie and Maxfield.

LITTLE HOUSE
The Laura Years

Collect all the

Little House
Chapter Books

❖ ❖ ❖

❖ ❖ ❖

US $4.25 / $5.95 CAN

ISBN 0-06-442077-9

HarperTroph
0
Cover art © 1998 by Renée G
Cover design by Alicia M